OLIVIA and her family are going to 's . **GRANDMA** **HOUSE** **OLIVIA** is excited to fly on a **PLANE** for the first time!

OLIVIA packs her TRUNK.
She packs CLOTHES and
her favorite toy.

6/11

OLIVIA™
Takes a Trip

adapted by Ellie O'Ryan
based on the screenplay "OLIVIA Takes a Road Trip"
written by Eric Shaw
illustrated by Jared Osterhold

Ready-to-Read

Simon Spotlight
New York   London   Toronto   Sydney

Based on the TV series *OLIVIA*™ as seen on Nickelodeon™

SIMON SPOTLIGHT
An imprint of Simon & Schuster Children's Publishing Division
1230 Avenue of the Americas, New York, New York 10020
Copyright © 2010 Silver Lining Productions Limited (a Chorion company). All rights reserved.
OLIVIA™ and © 2010 Ian Falconer. All rights reserved. All rights reserved, including the right of
reproduction in whole or in part in any form. SIMON SPOTLIGHT, READY-TO-READ,
and colophon are registered trademarks of Simon & Schuster, Inc.
For information about special discounts for bulk purchases, please contact Simon & Schuster
Special Sales at 1-866-506-1949 or business@simonandschuster.com.
Manufactured in the United States of America   1110 LAK
5 6 7 8 9 10
Library of Congress Cataloging-in-Publication Data
Bryant, Megan E.
Olivia takes a trip! / adapted by Megan E. Bryant ; illustrated by Jared Osterhold. — 1st ed.
p. cm. — (Ready-to-read)
"Based on the screenplay 'Olivia Takes a Road Trip' written by Eric Shaw."
"Based on the TV series 'Olivia' as seen on Nickelodeon"—T.p. verso.
ISBN 978-1-4169-9933-1
I. Osterhold, Jared, ill. II. Olivia (Television program) III. Title.
PZ7.B839801 2010
[E]—dc22
2009029213

 packs a small

IAN

LUNCH BOX

"This is my !"

SUITCASE

says.

IAN

 has some bad news.
A big  is coming.

STORM

The  cannot fly

PLANE

in the  .

STORM

They will drive the  CAR

to 🐷's 🏠 instead.
GRANDMA   HOUSE

🐷 is sad.
OLIVIA

She wanted to fly

on a ✈️ !
PLANE

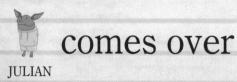 comes over

JULIAN

to say good-bye.

He has a present for .

OLIVIA

It is a !

WALKIE-TALKIE

and her family

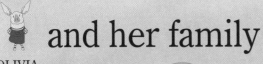

OLIVIA

get in the .

CAR

"Are we there yet?" asks.

IAN

The  is loud.
WALKIE-TALKIE
It wakes up  !
WILLIAM
 starts to cry.
WILLIAM

wishes she were

OLIVIA

on a .

PLANE

The  ride is boring.

CAR

At the helps
GAS STATION   OLIVIA   DAD

wash the ⬜ .
WINDSHIELD

 DAD 's brush has soap on it. But  OLIVIA 's brush has mud on it.  DAD has to wash the  WINDSHIELD again!

 buys an  for
MOM · ICE POP · OLIVIA

and  to share.
IAN

 wants the  part.
OLIVIA · RED

 wants the  part, too!
IAN · RED

The lands on the .
ICE POP · CAR

 has to wash the
DAD · WINDSHIELD

again.

"We will never get

to 's !" says.
GRANDMA · HOUSE · OLIVIA

has an idea.

OLIVIA

She will imagine

that she is on a !

PLANE

"Welcome to Air 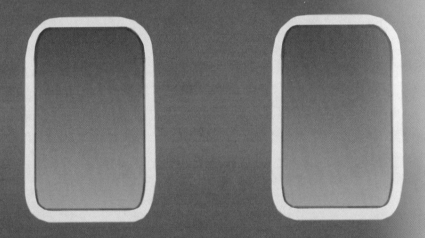 !"
OLIVIA

Captain OLIVIA says.

OLIVIA 's PLANE has a movie for DAD to watch. And POPCORN for DAD to eat. There is a yummy dinner for MOM.

And a 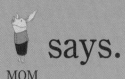 for , too.

RED ROSE   MOM

"This is the best  ever!"

PLANE

 says.

MOM

Captain  tells her family
OLIVIA
to put on their 🔶E🔶E .
SEAT BELTS
It is time to land the ✈ !
PLANE

Captain 🐷 sees dark ☁
OLIVIA   CLOUDS
out the window.

"Uh-oh!" says  .
OLIVIA

"Dark clouds mean

a  is coming."
STORM

"We will fly around the 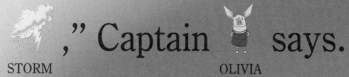 ," Captain says.

STORM   OLIVIA

The loops around a

PLANE

 .

RAINBOW

It flies past the  !
STORM

"We are at 's ."

GRANDMA   HOUSE

 shouts.

OLIVIA

She gives a big hug.

GRANDMA